Dabble Duck

by Anne Leo Ellis

ILLUSTRATED BY

Sue Truesdell

Harper & Row, Publishers

Dabble was a duck.
She was tiny and yellow and fluffy.
She lived in a cardboard box in Jason's room.
A light bulb kept her warm.
She splashed around in mash and water
(which was supposed to be her food)
and made an awful mess.

Dabble grew
and grew
and grew…

until she was no longer
tiny and yellow and fluffy,
but big and white and smooth.

Jason built a new home for her on the floor.

Dabble was like a big white pillow
with bright orange feet...
except when she had a bath in Jason's tub.

Then she looked scrawny
and bedraggled
until Jason wrapped her
in a big red towel
and she became
white and fluffy again.

Jason and Dabble took walks
and ran around the apartment
and quacked at each other.

But when Jason was at school,
Dabble was lonely.

When Jason came home,
Dabble was so glad to see him,
she almost knocked him down.
Jason was worried.
"Mommy, can we get another duck for Dabble?"
"No. I'm sorry, Jason, but Dabble is messier
than our whole family put together.
Think what two Dabbles would be like!
Maybe she'd be happier on a farm
with other ducks to play with."

"Dabble, you don't want to be with
other ducks if I'm not there,
do you?" said Jason.
"You're an apartment duck!
You wouldn't like
those silly country ducks anyway!"
Quack! Quack! Quack! said Dabble,
and wiggled her tail feathers.

The next day Jason's mother got on the phone
to find a new home for Dabble.
Jason took Dabble to the park.
Dabble followed Jason
down the hall
and into the elevator.

Flip, flop, flip,
slap, slap, slap
went her flat orange feet
on the smooth tiled floor.
Quack! Quack! Quack!
Everyone laughed and made room for her.
"It's Dabble," they said.
"Our apartment duck."

Jason and Dabble walked to the park.
"Look!" all the children yelled.
"There's Dabble!"
They ran over to pet her.
Jason sat on a bench and watched.
A little black dog was watching too.
His fur was tangled and dirty.
His right ear was torn.
But he sat with a big dog smile
and wagged his tail.

Learning
Resource
Center

When everyone had said hello to Dabble,
she waddled over to the little dog.
Quack! Quack! Quack! she said.
The little dog just sat and wagged his tail.
Quack! Quack! Quack!

"Dabble! Come on," called Jason. "Let's go!"
Quack! said Dabble one last time,
and followed Jason—
flip, flop, flip,
slap, slap, slap.

pretzels .50
Hotdog .75
Soda .75
peanuts .50
ice cream .45

The little black dog got up.
He pulled one leg close to his body
and hobbled after them.
When Jason stopped to buy a bag of peanuts,
Dabble chased pigeons.
The little dog hobbled after her
and tried to chase them too.
Suddenly he lay down
and rested.
He was panting.
Jason could see his ribs.
Jason went to him and stroked his head.
"Oh, dog, your leg must hurt a lot,
and you look hungry!
I think you need a friend."

The little dog licked Jason's hand
and tried to wag his tail.
"Come on, Dabble, let's take him home!"

Jason put the little dog on the bed in his room.
Dabble flapped her wings and hopped up too.
Jason got a bowl of bread and warm milk
from the kitchen.
The little dog lapped it up, and then
lay on the bed and slept and slept and slept
while Jason watched and worried and waited.
Dabble sat quietly waiting too.

Jason's mother opened the door.
"Hi, Jason, you're home.
Hi, Dabble!"
Then she saw the dog sleeping on the bed.
"Who's that?" she asked.
The little dog opened one eye
and then closed it again.

Jason told his mother what had happened.
His daddy came and listened too.
He stroked the little dog's tattered fur.
"He's hurt," said Jason's daddy.
"We need to take care of him," said his mother.
Jason's daddy went out to buy
bandages and dog food.

Dabble flapped her wings
and hopped back on the bed.
Quack! Quack! Quack!
she called to the little black dog.
The little dog opened both eyes
and looked at Dabble.
"Mommy! Look!
Dabble really loves him."
"Yes, Jason.
And I think he loves Dabble too.
They're going to be good friends."

"But I thought you said
we couldn't keep Dabble anymore."
"I know." She shrugged.
"And I even found a nice place for her
in the country.
Who knows? Maybe we'll have
to take her there someday.
Maybe we'll have to take both of them.
But for now let's keep her.
Let's keep both of them!"

Jason ran to Dabble
and scooped her up in his arms.
His mother picked up the little dog
and carried him to the bathroom.
She ran a tub of warm, bubbly water
that smelled of lilacs.
The little black dog had a bath.
Dabble had a swim, but not a bath.

When Jason's daddy returned,
the little dog ate a big bowl of dog food.
Dabble slopped around in her own dish
to keep him company.

Jason's daddy bandaged the little dog's ear
and put a splint on his leg.
Jason brushed his coat
until it was soft and fluffy
and gleamed like shiny black coal.

"Dabble's new dog needs a name,"
said Jason's mother.
"What'll we call him?" asked Jason,
settling down to think.
Quack! said Dabble,
nudging the little black dog with her bill.

"How about Fido?"
suggested Jason's daddy.
Quack! said Dabble.
She looked at the little black dog
and then at Jason.

"Mommy! Daddy!
Listen to Dabble!"
Quack! Quack! said Dabble,
nibbling the little dog's shiny fur.
Everyone stopped—and began to laugh.
"Dabble's right!"
Quack! said Dabble.
"Hi, Quack!" said Jason.
"Welcome home."
Quack smiled a big dog smile
and wagged his tail.

To Jonathan and Paul

Dabble Duck
Text copyright © 1984 by Anne Leo Ellis
Illustrations copyright © 1984 by Susan G. Truesdell
Printed in the U.S.A. All rights reserved.

Library of Congress Cataloging in Publication Data
Ellis, Anne Leo.
    Dabble duck.

    Summary: A lonesome pet duck finally solves her own
problem by befriending a bedraggled dog.
    [1. Ducks—Fiction.   2. Dogs—Fiction.   3. Friendship—
Fiction]   I. Truesdell, Sue, ill.   II. Title.
PZ7.E467Dab 1984   [E]   83-47692
ISBN 0-06-021817-7
ISBN 0-06-021818-5 (lib. bdg.)

Designed by Constance Fogler
1 2 3 4 5 6 7 8 9 10
First Edition